This Walker book belongs to:

_____

_____

To William

First published 2010 by Walker Books Ltd
87 Vauxhall Walk, London SE11 5HJ

This edition published 2011

10 9 8 7 6 5 4 3 2 1

© 2010 Petr Horáček

The right of Petr Horáček to be identified as author/illustrator of this work has been
asserted by him in accordance with the Copyright, Designs and Patents Act 1988

This book has been typeset in Little Grog

Printed in Thailand

British Library Cataloguing in Publication Data:
a catalogue record for this book is available from the British Library

ISBN 978-1-4063-3073-1

www.walker.co.uk

The Fly

Petr Horáček

WALKER BOOKS
AND SUBSIDIARIES
LONDON · BOSTON · SYDNEY · AUCKLAND

Two goggly eyes,
six hairy legs,
two transparent wings...

It's ME!
The House Fly.
But people don't like me
being in the house.

After breakfast I do my exercises... 156 times around

the lamp keeps me fit.

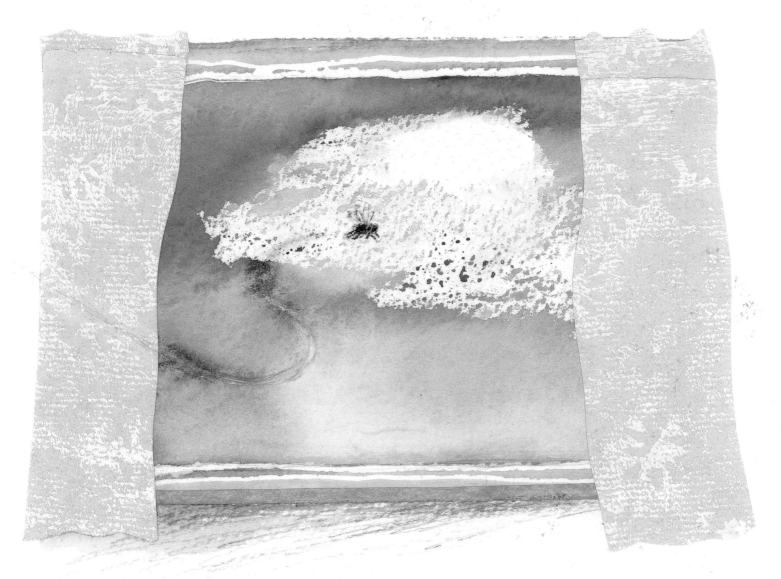

Then it's time for a snack.
I don't mind sharing, but he
doesn't want to share with me.
Flap! That was close!

Before lunch I always visit the cows.

But the animals don't really like me. I don't know why.

Once a frog nearly ate me,

then a bird nearly caught me.

Both in the same day.
Why?

I go back to the House for lunch.
I like my meals on time!

I can never understand ...

FLAP!

FLAP!

FLAP!

what the fuss is about.

FLAP!

Even when I find a good place to rest.

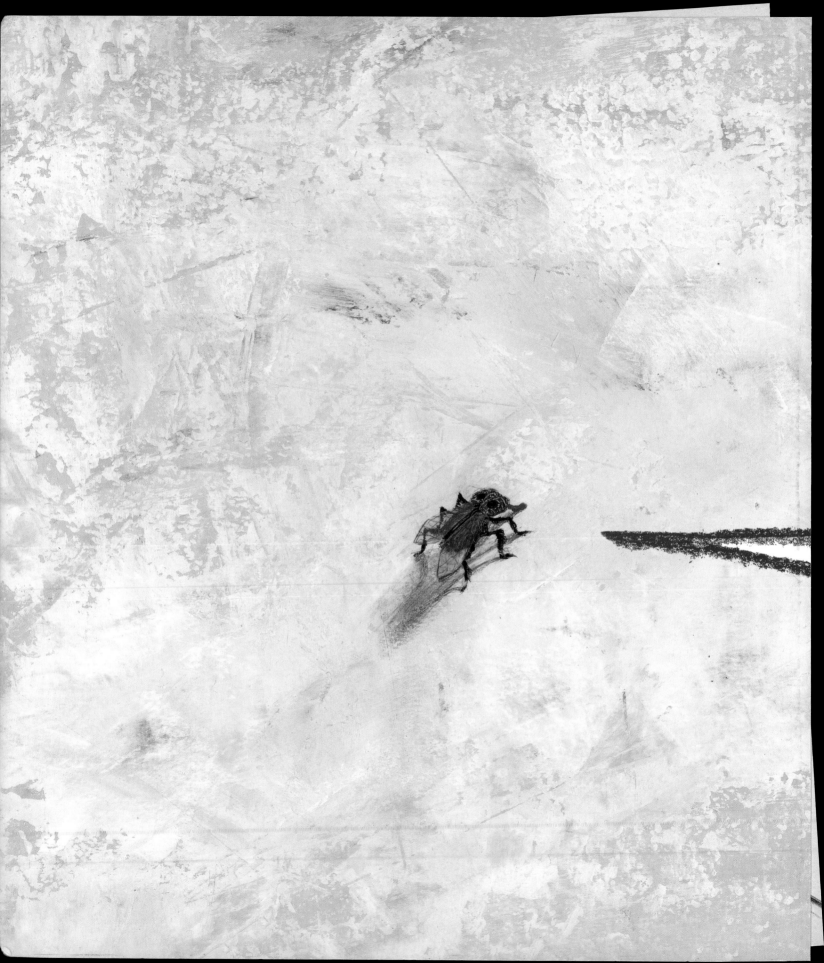

into trouble.

As you can see,
my life is not an easy one.
I'm just a simple creature.
I mean no harm to anyone.
So, if you see me, please be kind.
HEY, don't shut the book...

HELP... HELP... Do you
want to squash me?

Other books by Petr Horáček

Puffin Peter
ISBN 978-1-4063-2460-0

Look Out, Suzy Goose
ISBN 978-1-4603-1764-0

Suzy Goose and the Christmas Star
ISBN 978-1-4603-2621-5

Silly Suzy Goose
ISBN 978-1-4603-0458-9

Butterfly Butterfly
ISBN 978-1-84428-844-1

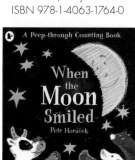

When the Moon Smiled
ISBN 978-0-7445-7047-2

A New House for Mouse
ISBN 978-1-4063-0122-9

Elephant
ISBN 978-1-4063-2441-9

This Little Cat
ISBN 978-1-4063-2511-9

Hello, Little Bird
ISBN 978-1-4063-2508-9

Run, Mouse, Run!
ISBN 978-1-4063-2509-6

Flutter by, Butterfly
ISBN 978-1-4063-2507-2

Beep Beep
ISBN 978-1-4063-2505-8

Choo Choo
ISBN 978-1-4063-2506-5

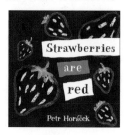

Strawberries are Red
ISBN 978-1-4063-2510-2

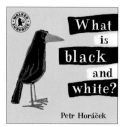

What is Black and White?
ISBN 978-1-4063-2512-6

Available from all good bookstores

www.walker.co.uk